TIMELINES ▶ World War II

Nathaniel Harris

ARCTURUS

This edition first published by Arcturus Publishing
Distributed by Black Rabbit Books
123 South Broad Street
Mankato
Minnesota MN 56001

Printed in China

Library of Congress Cataloging-in-Publication Data
Harris, Nathaniel, 1937-
  World War II / by Nathaniel Harris.
      p. cm. -- (Timelines)
Includes bibliographical references and index.
ISBN 978-1-84193-730-4 (alk. paper)
1. World War, 1939-1945--Juvenile literature. 2. World War, 1939-1945--
Chronology--Juvenile literature. I. Title. II. Title: World War 2. III. Title: World War
Two. IV. Series.

D743.7.H37 2007
940.53--dc22

                    2007007556

9 8 7 6 5 4 3 2

Series concept: Alex Woolf
Project manager and editor: Liz Miles
Designer: Simon Borrough
Picture researcher: Liz Miles
Consultant: James Vaughan
Cartography: The Map Studio

Picture credits:
Corbis: cover (Corbis), 4, 5 (Bettmann/Corbis), 7 (Corbis), 8 (Hulton-Deutsch
Collection/Corbis), 9 (Corbis), 10, 11 (Hulton-Deutsch Collection/Corbis), 14
(Corbis), 15 (Dmitri Baltermants/The Dmitri Baltermants Collection), 17 (Corbis),
19 (Corbis), 20, 21, 22 (Bettmann/Corbis), 23, 27 (Corbis), 28 (dpa/Corbis), 29
(Bettmann/Corbis), 30 (Bettmann/Corbis), 31 (Corbis), 32 (Hulton-Deutsch
Collection), 33, 34 (Corbis), 37 (Bettmann/Corbis), 38 (Hulton-Deutsch
Collection/Corbis), 39 (Bettmann/Corbis), 42 (Yevgeny Khaldei/Corbis), 43
(Bettmann/Corbis), 44 (Corbis), 45 (John Van Hasselt/Corbis Sygma).
TopFoto: 12, 13 (TopFoto), 18, 24 (Topham Picturepoint), 25 (TopFoto), 26
(Topham Picturepoint), 36 (2004 Topfoto), 40 (2005 Topfoto/AP), 41 (2004
TopFoto).

Contents

Munich Agreement

On this day, four leaders met and reached an agreement at Munich in southern Germany. They were Neville Chamberlain and Edouard Daladier, the prime ministers of Britain and France; the German dictator Adolf Hitler; and Benito Mussolini, dictator of Italy. The agreement ended a crisis that might have led to a European war.

The crisis was caused by German demands directed against Czechoslovakia (now separate states, the Czech Republic and Slovakia). Hitler claimed that the 3 million Germans who lived in Czechoslovakia were being persecuted; he demanded that the areas in which they lived should be transferred to Germany. Though alarmed by Hitler's attitude, neither Britain nor France wanted war. Chamberlain took the lead in negotiating personally with Hitler. Finally, the four-power meeting was arranged and Hitler got his way. The Czechs were told that they must give up large areas of their country, and they unwillingly obeyed.

CRISES OF THE 1930s

Munich was only one of several crises in the 1930s. Germany had lost World War I (1914–1918) and had been harshly treated by Britain, France, and the other victors. Hitler, German dictator from 1933, worked to restore Germany's position in Europe, but he also had his own grandiose plans of conquest. He rearmed Germany and

Leaders at the Munich conference. From left to right: Chamberlain, Daladier, and the dictators Adolf Hitler and Benito Mussolini.

scored a series of foreign policy triumphs based on righting real or imaginary wrongs done to Germany. Feeling that some German grievances were justified, the British and French followed a policy of appeasement (making concessions). Chamberlain believed that at Munich he had satisfied Hitler and secured "peace in our time."

CHANGING ATTITUDES

Most British and French people supported Chamberlain. But Hitler's next move started to change their minds. He engineered the breakup of Czechoslovakia and then bullied the Czechs into accepting German rule, disguised as a "protectorate." It was now obvious that Hitler was not just righting wrongs but was driving aggressively east. When he began to threaten Poland, Britain and France issued a guarantee that if Poland was attacked, they would come to its aid.

Fascism in Italy

From 1922, Benito Mussolini ruled Italy. His political doctrine, fascism, was strongly anti-democratic, glorifying the all-powerful leader, obedience to the state, and making war. Strength was good, weakness despicable.

THE RISE OF FASCISM

In the 1920s and 1930s, fascism found some followers in many countries. The most formidable were Hitler and his Nazi Party. The Nazi form of fascism included a poisonous racism. To Hitler, the Germans were a "master race" who should enslave "inferior" peoples, such as the Slavs of Eastern Europe, and wipe out supposedly evil groups—above all the Jews.

From 1931, Japan, similarly militaristic in outlook, waged a savage war of conquest against China. Germany, Italy, and Japan would become allies, known as the Axis. World War II would be, in part, a contest between fascism and democracy.

CROSS-REFERENCE WARS OF AGGRESSION: PAGES 6–7, 14–15, 16–17

German troops enter Czechoslovakia. They are being greeted with Nazi salutes by some of the country's German minority.

5

Germany Invades Poland

1 September 1939

At 4.45 a.m., German tanks, infantry, and aircraft surged across the frontiers into Poland and began an all-out attack. Britain and France demanded a German withdrawal, and when Hitler failed to respond, they declared war. Australia, New Zealand, Canada, and South Africa—all members of the British Commonwealth—joined the Allied (Anglo-French) side.

In reality, there was little they could do to help Poland in time. And Hitler had made sure that the only great power in Eastern Europe, the Soviet Union, would not oppose him. The majority of the Soviet Union's population was Russian, but the Soviet state was much larger than present-day Russia and had a long common border with Poland.

Europe in 1939, just before the German invasion of Poland on September 1. Also shown are Hitler's principal pre-war foreign policy triumphs.

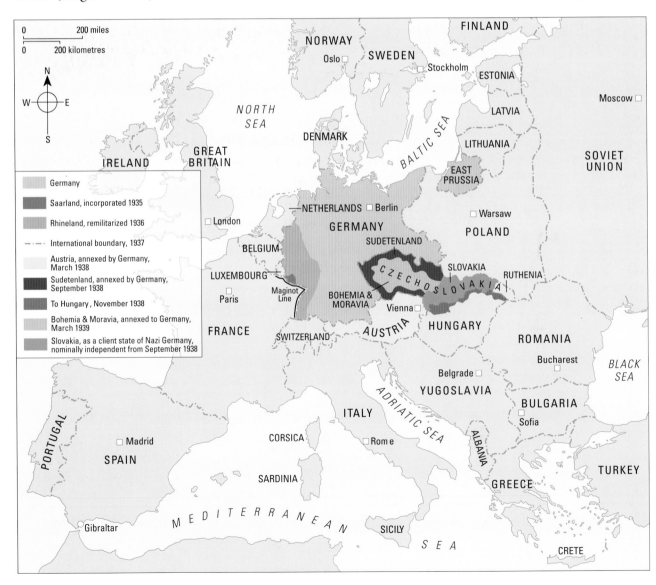

	Germany
	Saarland, incorporated 1935
	Rhineland, remilitarized 1936
–·–·–	International boundary, 1937
	Austria, annexed by Germany, March 1938
	Sudetenland, annexed by Germany, September 1938
	To Hungary, November 1938
	Bohemia & Moravia, annexed to Germany, March 1939
	Slovakia, as a client state of Nazi Germany, nominally independent from September 1938

NAZI-SOVIET PACT

All of the European powers were hostile to the Soviet Union because of its communist system, in which the state took over all property. Even when they became disillusioned with Hitler, Britain and France were slow to approach the Soviet Union. They relied on the fact that fascists and communists were deadly enemies. But Hitler saw his opportunity and astonished the world by coming to terms with the Soviet dictator, Joseph Stalin. Germany and the Soviet Union signed a non-aggression pact (neither would attack the other) and secretly agreed to divide Eastern Europe between them.

BLITZKRIEG!

The Poles fought bravely against the advancing Germans, but the campaign was over in weeks. In addition to having superior numbers, the Germans employed a devastating offensive technique, the *Blitzkrieg* (lightning war), based on rapid armored thrusts backed up by air strikes, which threw the opposing forces into disorder. Poland's situation was already desperate when the Red (Soviet) Army entered the country from the east.

Poland was partitioned between Germany and the Soviet Union. Over the next few months, the Soviets took control of the Baltic states and seized territory from Finland after a short but hard-fought war. But in the West, months passed with so little fighting that the period became known as "the Phoney War."

German troops, on motorcycles with sidecars, drive through a Polish village as their victorious army presses forward.

CROSS-REFERENCE CAMPAIGNS IN POLAND: PAGES 36–37, 38–39, 42–43

Germany Strikes in the West

On May 10, 1940, German armies thrust across the borders of the Low Countries (Holland, Belgium, and Luxembourg), all of them neutral states. The German objective was to push on into France, bypassing the Maginot Line of fortifications along France's eastern frontier. The Allies had anticipated such an attack, since the Phoney War had ended in April with a German occupation of neutral Denmark and Norway. French and British forces moved into Belgium to support the Belgian army.

THE BREAKTHROUGH

However, the Germans also broke through the Ardennes, a mountainous area in southwest Belgium. Their *Blitzkrieg* tactics were again brilliantly successful. Panzer (tank) divisions moved westward at great speed until they reached the French coast. They cut off the Allied forces in Belgium, which were driven back, trapped, and only evacuated from Dunkirk to Britain at a heavy cost.

Meanwhile, the German armies pressed relentlessly south, joined by fresh troops who had broken through the Maginot Line. Italy declared war on France and Britain and attacked in the south. Though allied with Hitler, Mussolini knew that Italy was weak and acted only when victory seemed certain. In the face of the German advance, the French government abandoned the capital, Paris, and on June 14 the Germans marched in.

FRANCE SURRENDERS

A new French prime minister took office. The aged Marshal Pétain was a hero of World War I, but he was now deeply defeatist. He immediately negotiated an armistice—in effect a French surrender. By its terms, Germany would continue to occupy northern France, while Pétain headed an authoritarian (non-democratic) regime at Vichy in the south. In theory, Vichy France remained independent, but it inevitably became a German puppet. Other French men and women chose to carry on the fight, joining the Free French

A German cavalry unit parades under the famous Arc de Triomphe in Paris, celebrating their victorious offensive.

TIMELINE	GERMAN VICTORIES 1940
April 9, 1940	▶ Germany invades Denmark and Norway. British and French forces, sent to help the Norwegians, withdraw on June 8.
May 10, 1940	▶ Germany invades the Low Countries.
May 12, 1940	▶ German forces cross the Meuse River into France.
May 20, 1940	▶ German armor reaches the French coast at Abbeville.
May 26, 1940	▶ Allied forces at Dunkirk begin an evacuation that lasts until June 4.
June 14, 1940	▶ German army enters Paris.
June 16, 1940	▶ Marshal Pétain becomes French prime minister.
June 22, 1940	▶ A German–French armistice is signed at Compiègne.
July 1, 1940	▶ France's government moves to Vichy.
July 3, 1940	▶ Britain destroys the French fleet in Algerian ports to prevent it from falling into German hands.

movement led by General Charles de Gaulle. Along with other exiles from occupied countries, they gathered in Britain, which now stood alone in Europe against Nazism.

CROSS-REFERENCE
PARIS LIBERATED:
PAGES 32–33

Dunkirk

The German advance from the Ardennes cut off 380,000 Allied soldiers, who fell back on the northern French coast. From May 26 to June 4 1940, over 200 Royal Navy ships and 800 civilian vessels evacuated troops from the beaches at Dunkirk. An official total of 338,226 men were saved; two-thirds were British, the rest French, Belgian, and Dutch. Approximately 40,000 French soldiers were left behind and became prisoners of war. The British suffered 68,000 casualties and abandoned hundreds of tanks and artillery pieces. Almost 250 vessels were lost in the evacuation. Britain had suffered a heavy defeat, but "the miracle of Dunkirk" enabled Britain to fight on.

British and French troops massed on the beach at Dunkirk. They wait to be taken off by sea before the German forces reach them.

Battle of Britain Begins

On July 10, 1940, the Luftwaffe (German Air Force) launched heavy bombing attacks on Britain's coastal shipping and its cities. This began the Battle of Britain, in which the Germans tried to achieve mastery of the skies before the start of an intended invasion. Fierce battles took place between the Spitfires and Hurricanes of the RAF (Royal Air Force) and German fighter planes escorting their bombers. In August and early September, the conflict reached its height when the Germans targeted the RAF's airfields and vital British industries.

GERMANY'S FIRST SETBACK

Though under almost unbearable strain, the RAF held on, and the Germans were the first to change their tactics, carrying out devastating bombings of London. But a huge assault on September 15 (Battle of Britain Day) cost the Luftwaffe 185 planes, a loss so severe that it abandoned daytime raids. In effect, Germany admitted defeat in the battle for control of the air—its first notable setback of the war.

THE BLITZ

Worse ordeals faced Britain's citizens. The Luftwaffe no longer dueled with the RAF, but it intensified its attacks on cities and ports, flying by night. During "the Blitz," high explosives, parachute mines, and incendiary bombs rained down on London, Coventry, Plymouth, and many other cities; even the Clydeside in Scotland and Belfast in Northern Ireland proved to be in range. After May 1941, the Blitz diminished, mainly because the Germans were preparing a new war, against the Soviet Union. There were still periodic bombings, and in 1944–1945 a new terror appeared in the form of unmanned "flying bombs," the V-1 and V-2.

A Spitfire patrol takes off. Fast and highly maneuverable, the Spitfire played a decisive role in the Battle of Britain.

London in the Blitz

"The house about 30 yards from ours struck at one in the morning by a bomb. Completely ruined. Another bomb in the square still unexploded . . . The house was still smouldering. That is a great pile of bricks. Underneath all the people who had gone down to their shelter. Scraps of cloth hanging to the bare walls at the side still standing . . . **Who lived there?** I suppose the casual young men and women I used to see from my window; the flat dwellers who used to have flower pots and sit in the balcony. All now blown to bits."

From the diary notes of writer Virginia Woolf, for September 10, 1940.
Anne Olivier Bell, ed., *The Diary of Virginia Woolf*, vol. 5, 1936–1941 (Hogarth Press, 1984).

By the end of the war, Britain's cities were badly scarred, 62,000 civilians had been killed, and a third of its homes had been damaged or destroyed. But the Blitz did not demoralize the population or destroy British industries and communications. Inspired by a new leader, Winston Churchill, Britain, more than any other country, organized every aspect of the national life to endure and win the war.

CROSS-REFERENCE BOMBING CAMPAIGNS: PAGES 20–21, 34–35, 44–45

A German bomber goes into action over land near London's docks.

Sinking of the *Bismarck*

27 MAY 1941

A dramatic naval engagement began when the Germans' greatest battleship, the gigantic *Bismarck*, left the Norwegian port of Bergen with the cruiser *Prince Eugen*. They were headed for the Atlantic, their mission to destroy Allied shipping. The *Bismarck* was spotted, and a strong British force closed in. But when the *Hood* and the *Prince of Wales* engaged the German warships, the *Bismarck* scored a direct hit on the *Hood*. It sank in minutes, taking over 1,400 men with it. The *Bismarck* escaped but was sighted again by a British flying boat. On May 26, planes from the aircraft carrier *Ark Royal* attacked with torpedoes, and one hit the *Bismarck's* rudder. The next day, the crippled giant was pounded by British ships until it sank. Only 110 of its 2,300-strong crew were saved.

BATTLE OF THE ATLANTIC
The destruction of the *Bismarck* was part of the "Battle of the Atlantic," in which the Axis hoped to defeat Britain by cutting off vital supplies from the still-neutral U.S. Britain's navy was more powerful than Germany's surface fleet, and after the loss of the *Bismarck*, Germany's remaining heavy ships withdrew to safer European waters.

However, Germany had other means of waging war in the Atlantic— aircraft, mines, and above all the U-boats (submarines), which gathered in "wolf packs" and torpedoed Allied merchant vessels and warships. After the U.S. and the Soviet Union joined the Allies in 1941, American vessels were also targeted, as were convoys

The Bismarck *takes a direct hit. This dramatic photograph was taken by a sailor on a sister German vessel, the* Prince Eugen.

October 14, 1939	▶ The battleship *Royal Oak* is torpedoed by a U-boat in Scapa Flow.
December 13, 1939	▶ Battle of the River Plate: the damaged German cruiser *Graf Spee* seeks refuge in Montevideo (Uruguay). On December 17, it is scuttled (disabled by its own crew).
March 6, 1941	▶ Churchill's "Battle of the Atlantic" directive gives this sector highest priority.
May 27, 1941	▶ British planes and warships sink the *Bismarck*.
October 1942	▶ The British navy captures Enigma equipment and code books on a sinking U-boat.
March 16, 1943	▶ U-boats sink 22 ships belonging to two convoys—the peak of their success.
May 1943	▶ "Black May": 40 U-boats are destroyed and the Battle of the Atlantic turns decisively against the Germans.

bringing supplies to the Soviet Union's far-northern ports on the perilous "Murmansk run."

WINNING THE BATTLE

Enormous quantities of shipping were sunk by the U-boats, peaking in March 1943. But the losses were made up by extraordinary U.S. feats in building "Liberty ships," and the U-boat menace was gradually mastered. The Allies broke Germany's Enigma code and directed convoys away from wolf-pack areas. New sonar devices made it easier to locate and destroy U-boats. Allied warships and radar-equipped aircraft took a heavy toll. Although they fought on, by late 1943, the Germans had clearly lost the Battle of the Atlantic.

CROSS-REFERENCE
WAR AT SEA: PAGES
22–23, 34–35

A German submarine on the surface, safe for the time being from attack by air or sea. The U-boats led a precarious existence.

U-boats

Submarines became the Germans' principal weapon in their struggle to break Allied supply lines in the Atlantic. In 1939, there were only 57 in service, but another 900 were added in the course of the war. At any one time, their maximum strength was about 450, but in the Atlantic alone, they sank 175 Allied warships and 2,500 merchant vessels. Understandably, U-boats were described as "iron coffins": 28,000 of the 40,000 men who served in them were killed.

Germany Invades the USSR

The onslaught—"Operation Barbarossa"—began at dawn, without a declaration of war. Three million German soldiers attacked on a front stretching from the Baltic to the Black Sea. The Soviet forces were taken completely by surprise. Stalin, the Soviet dictator, had received warnings that an invasion was imminent but refused to believe them.

The stunned Soviet forces suffered huge losses, including 1,800 aircraft, during the first days of the campaign. German mechanized divisions raced ahead, using their practiced *Blitzkrieg* tactics, and scored brilliant successes. Entire Soviet armies were encircled and destroyed. By September, the great southern cities of the Ukraine, Kiev and Kharkov, had fallen. In the north, Leningrad was cut off and besieged, and in central Russia, the Germans were advancing toward the Soviet capital, Moscow.

Winter assault

"On 13 November , we awoke and shivered. . . . The icy winds from Siberia—the breath of death—were blowing across the steppes. . . . Those Arctic blasts that had taken us by surprise in our protected positions had scythed through our attacking troops. In a couple of days there were **100,000 casualties from frost-bite alone. . . .** More and more reports were . . . recommending that the attack on Moscow by a summer-clad army be abandoned, and that winter positions be prepared . . . The order persisted: 'Attack!' And our soldiers attacked."

Medical officer Hans Haape records the impact of the Russian winter on the advance of the German armies. Hans Haape, *Moscow Tram Stop* (Collins, 1957).

MASTER OF EUROPE

Hitler was close to becoming master of all Europe. Most of the Balkan (southeast European) states had become his allies, and in April 1941, Germany had swiftly conquered Yugoslavia and also Greece, which Hitler's Italian allies had attacked with humiliating lack of success. The Soviet Union was different, if only because of its huge size, manpower reserves, and harsh winters, which had ruined earlier invaders. Hitler calculated that he could win by conquering all of European Russia, as far as the Ural Mountains, before the winter set in.

But German difficulties were mounting. Even victorious advances were exhausting over such vast

A German tank advances toward the border as part of the Nazi invasion of the Soviet Union, launched on June 22, 1941.

A Soviet soldier throws a grenade. Despite catastrophic defeats, the Soviet Union proved harder to conquer than Hitler had anticipated.

distances, and German units had to rest and be resupplied. Soviet resistance was stiffening, and Stalin proclaimed a "scorched earth" policy of destroying everything useful in the path of the enemy. However, much of Soviet industry was saved by dismantling and transporting hundreds of factories to safe places behind the lines.

WINTER'S GRIP

In November, the weather began to deteriorate. German units reached the suburbs of Moscow, but by early December, winter had closed in. Counterattacks by newly arrived Soviet armies reinforced the message that the Germans had failed to deliver a knockout blow and had a long, hard struggle before them.

CROSS-REFERENCE THE WAR IN THE SOVIET UNION: PAGES 28–29, 36–37

Japan Attacks Pearl Harbor

7 DECEMBER 1941

Just before 8 a.m., the first wave of Japanese aircraft hit the U.S. Pacific Fleet in Pearl Harbor. For two hours Japanese torpedo planes, bombers, divebombers, and Zero fighters sank or damaged eight battleships and 10 other vessels. Air bases were put out of action and hundreds of planes destroyed on the ground. About 2,400 Americans were killed. Having achieved total surprise, the Japanese lost only 29 aircraft.

A HIGH-RISK OPERATION

Pearl Harbor was on the Hawaiian island of Oahu. The attacking planes had been brought in range of their target by a Japanese fleet that had sailed across the north Pacific. The fleet escaped detection and so did the planes when they set off on their mission from aircraft carriers. The Japanese had enjoyed good luck, but American lack of vigilance also contributed to the disaster.

This was surprising, since U.S.–Japanese relations were already tense. Japan was an aggressive power, intent on conquering China and dominating eastern Asia. The U.S. opposed Japanese ambitions, eventually cutting

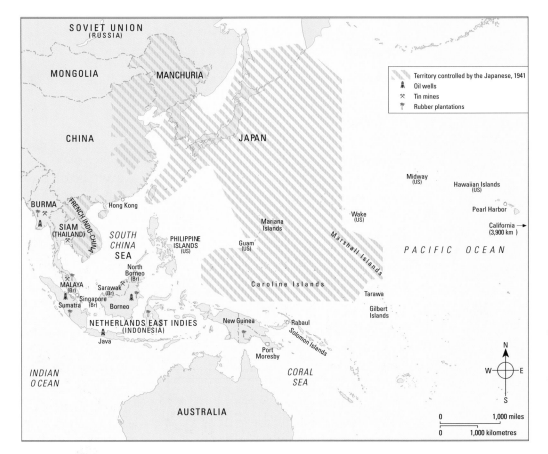

Japan's empire in 1941, just before the attack at Pearl Harbor. Also marked are the vital raw materials of Southeast Asia, which the Japanese would seize.

off supplies of essential raw materials to Japan. Without oil in particular, the Japanese war machine would grind to a halt. But plentiful resources could be had in Southeast Asia if the U.S. could be prevented from interfering by, for example, eliminating its Pacific Fleet. Japanese–American talks were still taking place when Pearl Harbor was attacked. The same day, Japanese forces landed in Malaya and Thailand, and Japanese aircraft hit U.S. bases in the Philippines and the Pacific.

THE WORLD AT WAR

The Japanese strike had another consequence: Germany and Italy declared war on the U.S. Hitler was already angry with the U.S. because, although technically neutral, President Franklin D. Roosevelt openly sympathized with the Allies and gave them substantial help. Even so, the Axis declarations were a blunder. Like the Japanese, they grossly underestimated U.S. determination and industrial might. In the world war, the balance of resources was now decisively in the Allies' favor. However long the struggle, its outcome was certain.

CROSS-REFERENCE
JAPANESE
EXPANSION: PAGES
18–19

Huge columns of smoke pour from the stricken U.S. ships, destroyed while still in their berths at Pearl Harbor.

Singapore Falls

Singapore was Britain's strongest military and naval base in the Far East, an island city at the southern tip of Malaya (present-day Malaysia). Since it was strategically placed to interfere with Japan's thrust into Southeast Asia, the Japanese landed troops on the east coast of Malaya and drove south. The two British warships in the area, the *Prince of Wales* and *Repulse*, were sunk by Japanese planes—a further example of the role that air power now played in war at sea.

A SWIFT VICTORY

The Japanese troops were battle hardened and had a daunting superiority in tanks and aircraft. Though Malaya was defended by substantial British and Commonwealth forces, the Japanese advanced with astonishing speed, and by January 30 the Allies had retreated to Singapore. The island was bombarded by land and sea. Then, on the night of February 8, the Japanese stormed across the strait separating it from the mainland and the defenders fell back, concentrating in the city of Singapore. They still had over 100,000 men, but water was running out. The British commander, General Percival, did not realize that the Japanese were short of ammunition, and on 15 February he accepted the Japanese demand for an unconditional surrender.

JAPAN'S CONQUESTS

The fall of Singapore, with no heroic last stand, was a shattering blow to British prestige in the East, where Britain had a huge empire. But the British were not the only victims of the triumphant Japanese. They captured U.S.-held Guam and Wake Island, completing a ring of Pacific island defenses from which Japan hoped to hold back any U.S. attack. They conquered the Philippines, though only after a grimly determined American resistance at Bataan and Corregidor that lasted until May 1942. By May, the Japanese had won the Battle of the Java Sea and occupied the Dutch East Indies (now Indonesia), securing badly needed oil supplies. They had taken most of Burma and were advancing in New Guinea. With British India and Australia under threat, Japan reached the height of its good fortune.

Victorious Japanese troops parade in Singapore after capturing the island city and the Allied army that defended it.

After the surrender

"When we entered Singapore we were surprised to see that the airfields, harbour and city had not been destroyed by the enemy. Seizing a junior enemy officer, we questioned him. 'Why did you not destroy Singapore?' we asked. 'Because we shall return again,' he replied. Again, we asked, 'Don't you believe Britain is beaten in this war?' He replied, 'We may be defeated ninety-nine times, but in the final round we will be all right—**we will win .**'"

This encounter is described by Japanese commander Colonel Masanobu Tsuji, who planned the assault on Singapore. Colonel Masanobu Tsuji, *Japan's Greatest Victory: Britain's Worst Defeat* (Spellmount, 1997).

CROSS-REFERENCE JAPANESE WARRIOR CODE: PAGES 34–35

The Bataan death march. Thousands of starving and exhausted U.S. and Filipino prisoners died on a forced march of more than 50 miles (80 km).

Thousand Bomber Raid

The raid was directed against Cologne, a famous German cathedral city and industrial center. The RAF gathered almost every bomber it possessed to put a force of 1,047 planes into the air, making Operation Millennium the first thousand-bomber raid of the war. During the night attack on Cologne, 1,454 tons of bombs were dropped; two-thirds of them were incendiaries, and the fires they started were visible from the air 150 miles (240 km) away. About 480 people were killed, over 5,000 injured, and almost 5,000 made homeless. The destruction, less lasting than was believed at the time, was still impressive. Several thousand buildings were destroyed or damaged, including hundreds of industrial facilities. The RAF lost 42 aircraft.

SATURATION BOMBING

By this time, the war in the air had undergone great changes. In 1941, the results of raiding over Europe had been disappointing. But by 1942, more powerful bombers and other improvements had transformed RAF prospects. A new commander in chief, Arthur Harris, was convinced that bombing alone, if sufficiently intensive, could win the war. The raid on Cologne, followed by a similar attack on Essen, marked the beginning of a strategy of saturation bombing. Such offensives became more intense as the USAAF (U.S. airforce) began to operate from British bases.

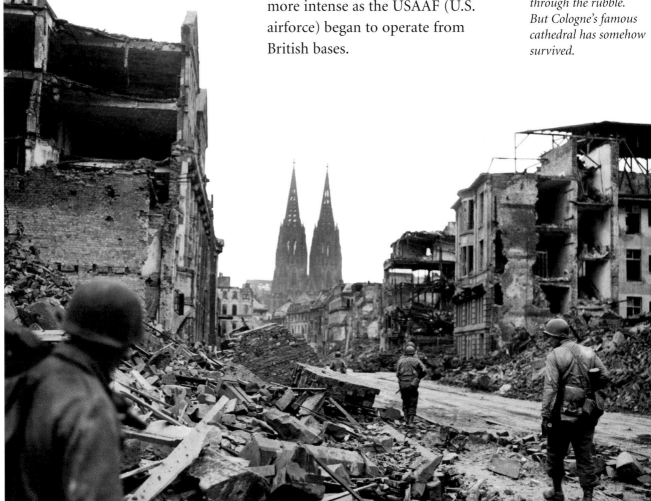

Devastated Cologne: US troops advance through the rubble. But Cologne's famous cathedral has somehow survived.

ALLIED BOMBING OF EUROPE 1942–1945

February 1942
▶ "Bomber" Harris becomes commander-in-chief of RAF Bomber Command. USAAF establishes its British headquarters.

May 30, 1942
▶ The Thousand Bomber raid on Cologne.

August 27, 1942
▶ The USAAF carries out its first raid on occupied Europe, over Rouen, France.

January 27, 1943
▶ The USAAF carries out its first operations over Germany, bombing Wilhelmshaven.

May 17, 1943
▶ Three-month-long Allied bombing of the Ruhr. British aircraft—the "Dambusters"—breach the Mohne and Eder dams with special "bouncing bombs."

February 13–14, 1945
▶ Allied bombing destroys the historic city of Dresden; at least 40,000 die. This becomes the most controversial Allied action of the war.

GERMANY IN RUINS

In 1943, the Allies saturation-bombed Germany in earnest. The Ruhr, Hamburg, and the German capital, Berlin, were bombed night after night for weeks. Allied casualties were heavy, but they, unlike the Axis, were able to replace losses in crews and aircraft. In 1944, Allied air superiority helped to ensure the success of the Normandy landings. By then, the Allies were bombing Germany in huge sorties, almost without opposition. German war production held up surprisingly well for a long time, leading to some postwar questioning of the Allies' strategy. But enemy communications were crippled, and by the end of the war, Hitler's Germany lay in ruins.

CROSS-REFERENCE BOMBING GERMANY: PAGES 42–43

Allied incendiary bombs cast sinister shadows as they fall on the German city of Hanover.

Pilot's-eye view

"Already, only twenty-three minutes after the attack had started, Cologne was ablaze from end to end, and the main force of the attack was still to come. . . . Every now and then . . . **something would fall burning from the heavens**: German or British? We could not tell which; only hope. . . . Thirteen thousand feet below, the covering intruder force had swung into action . . . We watched the snuffing out of searchlights and the strafing of aerodromes and said with thankfulness: 'Here at last is the first bomber battle, and the bombers are winning.'"

Cologne as seen by bomber pilot Leonard Cheshire, who won Britain's highest-ranking medal, the Victoria Cross.
Leonard Cheshire, VC., *Bomber Pilot* (Hutchinson, 1943).

Battle of Midway Begins

The Battle of Midway was intended to be Japan's second masterstroke against the U.S. navy. Almost the entire Japanese fleet was mobilized for an offensive that would capture Midway Island, extending Japan's defensive perimeter a further 1864 miles (3,000 km) into the central Pacific. To fool the Americans, Japanese forces would mount a diversionary attack on the Aleutians, a U.S. island chain south-west of Alaska. When the U.S. fleet did sail to relieve Midway, the superior Japanese forces would crush it.

INSIDE INFORMATION

Unknown to the Japanese, the Americans had cracked the enemy's radio codes. They knew about the attack on Midway, and the Pacific Fleet headed toward it. Since the Japanese had divided their ships into several groups, the Americans were able to tackle the main invasion force on more or less equal terms. The attacks were again conducted mostly by carrier-borne aircraft, but the Americans were helped by additional planes stationed on Midway.

4 JUNE 1942

The balance of naval strength in the Pacific, 1942–1945

Figures refer to the beginning of each year.

		1942	1943	1944	1945
Battleships	U.S.	0	9	13	23
	Japan	10	10	9	5
Aircraft carriers	U.S.	3	2	7	14
	Japan	6	4	4	2
Escort carriers	U.S.	0	4	22	65
	Japan	4	3	4	2
Cruisers	U.S.	16	25	30	45
	Japan	38	36	37	16
Destroyers	U.S.	40	146	245	296
	Japan	112	99	77	40

The Battle of Midway. Heavy anti-aircraft fire fails to protect the U.S. carrier Yorktown *from sinking after intensive Japanese attacks.*

The crucial moment in the battle came when U.S. torpedo bombers were virtually wiped out by Japanese fighters. Immediately afterward, while the Zeros were refueling and rearming on the carrier decks, U.S. dive bombers swooped down from the clouds and hit them with devastating effect. At the end of the day, the battered Japanese accepted defeat and withdrew.

A TURNING POINT

A month earlier, the Japanese had received a check at the indecisive Battle of the Coral Sea, abandoning an intended attack on Port Moresby in New Guinea. But Midway was much more serious and marked a turning point in the war at sea. The Japanese lost four carriers and 332 aircraft, along with their best front-line pilots. The two sides were now more evenly matched, and over the following year the advantage steadily passed to the U.S. as it produced more and more ships, planes, and trained pilots. The wearing away of Japanese naval strength continued through the Guadalcanal campaign (pages 24–25) and culminated in 1944 with overwhelming victories in the two battles of the Philippine Sea.

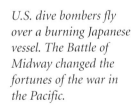

CROSS-REFERENCE THE PACIFIC WAR: PAGES 24–25, 34–35

U.S. dive bombers fly over a burning Japanese vessel. The Battle of Midway changed the fortunes of the war in the Pacific.

U.S. Marines Land on Guadalcanal

When the First Marine Division landed, the Japanese were consolidating their position on the Solomon Islands by constructing an airstrip on Guadalcanal, one of the southern group. This, the first Allied land offensive of the Pacific War, began well as the marines established a beachhead and seized the airstrip. The small nearby island of Tulagi was captured, but only after most of its garrison of 1,500 defenders were dead.

The following night, a Japanese force hit back, sinking four Allied cruisers and damaging three other vessels in a surprise attack (the Battle of Savo Island). A ferocious six-month struggle began. Both sides made great efforts to reinforce their troops on Guadalcanal. Naval and air support played a vital role in protecting or attacking transports and shelling enemy positions. Each side ended by losing 24 vessels, but the Japanese sustained very heavy losses on land and in the air. More successfully reinforced and supplied, the U.S. forces drove back the outnumbered Japanese, who finally evacuated Guadalcanal early in February 1943.

WAR IN PAPUA

Another long, hard campaign was fought in Papua, the easternmost region of New Guinea. The Japanese planned to march over the mountains and take Port Moresby on the southern coast, 300 miles (480 km) from northern Australia. They were finally forced to withdraw on September 17, and were driven from Papua in November 1942.

AMERICAN STRATEGY

After their failure in the Guadalcanal and Papua campaigns, the Japanese were forced on the defensive, desperately intent on preventing the Allies from reaching their home islands. American strategy was now based on a two-pronged advance. In the southwest Pacific, led by General

U.S. soldiers count the bodies of their Japanese enemies, killed in the fight for the airstrip on Guadalcanal.

MacArthur, they fought their way through the Solomons and New Guinea until they had the Philippines in their sights. And in the central Pacific, under Admiral Nimitz, they took one island group after another. This "island hopping" punched a gaping hole in Japan's defensive perimeter and brought the Americans menacingly close to Tokyo.

CROSS-REFERENCE
US LANDINGS:
PAGES **30–31, 32–33, 34–35**

Passions of war

"I . . . heard a loud blubbering shout, like a turkey gobbler's cry, followed by a burst of shooting. I hit the deck immediately. . . . When . . . there was no more shooting, I walked to the . . . top of the ridge, and found two bodies of Japs there—and one marine. Gunner Banta told me that three Japs had made a suicide charge with bayonets. One of them had spitted the marine, and had been shot. A second had been tackled and shot and the third had run away. . . . **The animal-like cry I had heard had been a Jap 'Banzai!' shout.***"*

The hatred and prejudice born of war are clear in journalist Richard Tregaskis's account of an incident on Guadalcanal.

Quoted in Richard J. Aldrich, *The Faraway War* (Doubleday, 2005).

War in the jungle: a Red Cross unit carries a sick U.S. soldier across a stream during the campaign in New Guinea.

Victory at El Alamein

A German tank crew surrenders to Allied troops at El Alamein, where the Axis forces in North Africa were finally driven back.

At 9:40 p.m., a thousand heavy guns opened up, lighting the night sky over the Western Desert. Engineers cleared paths through the enemy minefields and the infantry advanced, engaging in bloody hand-to-hand fighting, followed by the tanks of the Eighth Army. At El Alamein in Egypt, British and Commonwealth and Free French forces made their supreme effort to crush a tough and resourceful enemy.

The Axis troops were badly shaken, and on October 25 their commander, Erwin Rommel, flew back from Germany to take over. But even the legendary "Desert Fox" could not hold a foe attacking in overwhelming strength. On November 2, after a final attempt to counterattack, Rommel gave the order to withdraw. His men were pursued by the Eighth Army all along the Libyan coastline and into Tunisia, a Vichy French colony.

NORTH AFRICAN CAMPAIGNS

El Alamein was the final battle in the desert and East African campaigns that began in July 1940, shortly after Italy entered the war. Allied troops captured all of Italy's East African possessions and took huge numbers of prisoners. The Italian position in Libya was also crumbling when Rommel arrived in March 1941 with two German divisions, the famous Afrika Korps. For over a year, the Axis and Allied armies advanced and retreated over vast distances. With relatively small forces, Rommel outmaneuvered his enemies and in May 1942 even drove the Allies back to El Alamein, 62 miles (100 km) from the British naval base at Alexandria. But then a new Eighth Army commander, Bernard Montgomery, methodically gathered reinforcements and planned the overwhelming assault that ended Axis resistance.

The battle begins

"From far back . . . a tongue of flame leapt out. The first gun had fired. For a split second all was dark again. We heard the sergeant shout, his voice . . . wild, loud, excited: 'Fire!' The whole horizon to the east spewed heavenwards in a fount of orange and blood-red flame, stabbing at the sky. The thunder of the barrage . . . struck us, a tidal wave of sound; it hammered on our ear drums and whipped our shirts against our chests . . . I could hear nothing but the crashing thunder of the barrage, thunder born of flame that was the horizon and the sky and the whole earth."

A gripping account by Australian Private J. A. Crawford. Quoted in Niall Barr, *Pendulum of War: The Three Battles of El Alamein* (Pimlico, 2005).

OPERATION TORCH

Meanwhile, the Allies were striking another blow in North Africa: Operation Torch, commanded by U.S. general Dwight D. Eisenhower. A huge fleet landed mainly U.S. troops in Morocco and Algeria. These were French colonies controlled by agents of the Vichy regime, who put up little resistance. But the Germans rushed troops into Tunisia, the obvious jumping-off point for an invasion of Italy. After a long, punishing struggle, the Germans surrendered in May 1943, leaving all of North Africa in Allied hands.

CROSS-REFERENCE
TANK BATTLES: PAGES 28–29, 40–41

Field Marshal Rommel in his car, somewhere in the Western Desert. Rommel proved to be one of the war's ablest commanders.

Surrender at Stalingrad

On January 31, 1943, the German commander in the Soviet city of Stalingrad, Field Marshal Friedrich Paulus, surrendered to soldiers of the Red Army. Within two days, all German resistance ended. Over 90,000 half-starved, frostbitten Axis soldiers shuffled into captivity.

THE GERMAN OFFENSIVE

The capitulation ended the ambitious offensive launched in July 1942 by the Germans and their Italian and Romanian allies. Instead of attacking Leningrad or Moscow, they struck on the southern front. Army Group South headed for the oilfields of the Caucasus. Army Group North drove toward the Volga River. By August, it was approaching Stalingrad, on the west bank of the Volga, and the Luftwaffe was pounding it mercilessly.

Soon the city was encircled and besieged. An epic struggle began in which every house was fought over, sometimes changing hands several times a day. Because of its links with Stalin, the city became a symbolic prize to both sides. By October, the Germans had taken most of Stalingrad, but supplies were short and the Soviets were preparing a powerful counterattack.

Exhausted, frozen, and hungry: soldiers of the surrounded German Sixth Army surrender to Soviet forces at the Battle of Stalingrad.

To the death

The war on the Eastern Front was a savage and titanic struggle. The Nazis behaved with incredible barbarity, inspiring the Soviet people with an equally ferocious determination. Losses were horrific. In 1941, 4 million Soviet troops were killed or captured; the German figure was 1,110,000. But Soviet reserves were huge, and German casualties mattered more in the long run. At Stalingrad, the Germans and their allies lost 800,000 men as well as the 90,000 who surrendered. At the war's end, the German dead on all fronts numbered about 3.3 million. On their front, at least 8.6 million Soviet servicemen died; massacre and starvation accounted for at least another 7 million civilian deaths.

A DOOMED ARMY

It came on November 19. Fresh Russian divisions from the Moscow sector attacked and began to encircle the besiegers. Hitler refused to allow a withdrawal, and the Axis forces were incapable of breaking out. An attempt to relieve them failed, and the Luftwaffe proved unable to drop enough supplies. By late January, the onetime besiegers were penned into the ruined city. Despite Hitler's demands for a fight to the death, Paulus finally surrendered.

CROSS-REFERENCE STREET FIGHTING: PAGES 38–39, 42–43

Nevertheless, in spring 1943 the Germans launched a successful new offensive. Then both sides built up their forces for another showdown. At Kursk, on the southern front, they fought the greatest tank battle in history. The battlefield became a wasteland of burned-out armor and mangled corpses. Losses were enormous, but in the end the Germans were forced to withdraw.

The tide of war had now definitely turned. The Soviets had the upper hand, and the Germans were forced permanently on the defensive.

As the battle for Stalingrad reaches its climax, Soviet troops move forward through the rubble on the outskirts of the city.

Invasion of Sicily

10 JULY 1943

On July 10, 1943, a 2,000-strong Allied armada landed 160,000 troops on the south coast of Sicily, the large Italian island close to the mainland. Italian resistance was feeble, and at first Allied progress was rapid. But German units fought a hard delaying action before successfully evacuating the island in mid-August.

THE FALL OF MUSSOLINI

The invasion had an immediate impact on Italian politics. For Mussolini the war had been a series of humiliations. His armies had failed almost everywhere, and the invasion was the last straw. His followers turned on the once all-powerful leader. He was dismissed and arrested, and the Fascist Party was dissolved. A new prime minister, Marshal Pietro Badoglio, publicly upheld the German alliance but secretly negotiated a surrender to the Allies.

The Germans were not fooled. They took over the country before the Italians could reorganize, and a daring, glider-borne rescue freed Mussolini from prison. Meanwhile, on September 3, Allied forces crossed the Strait of Messina and secured a foothold on mainland Italy, followed by U.S. landings in much greater numbers at Salerno. German

The Allied invasion of Sicily: U.S. soldiers wade ashore from landing craft.

Coming ashore

"The moment I put my foot on land two enemy fighters, their machine-guns blazing away, skimmed overhead. I got awful wet diving under a low over-hanging ledge in the cliff at the same time as a wave. We climbed the bank, cut the wire and ran across a vine-yard to the road. Odd rounds of rifle fire did nothing to slow us down. . . . There was a thick wood to the left of the road and from each tree hung a dead allied paratrooper (Americans I think). It was weird, **we could only leave them there.**"

British private Ernest Kerans of the Ninth Durham Light Infantry on landing at Sicily.
Quoted in Field Marshal Lord Carver, *The Imperial War Museum Book of the War in Italy 1943–1945* (Sidgwick and Jackson, 2001).

TIMELINE	**THE WAR IN ITALY 1943–1945**
July 10, 1943	▶ The Allies invade Sicily.
July 25, 1943	▶ Mussolini is dismissed and arrested.
September 3, 1943	▶ Allied forces under Montgomery land at Reggio, southern Italy.
September 8, 1943	▶ The Italian surrender, agreed on September 3, is announced.
September 10, 1943	▶ The main Allied invasion force lands at Salerno.
September 12, 1943	▶ German troops rescue Mussolini.
January 22, 1944	▶ U.S. forces land at Anzio.
May 18, 1944	▶ Monte Cassino falls.
June 4, 1944	▶ Allied troops enter Rome.
April 28, 1945	▶ Attempting to escape to Switzerland, Mussolini is captured and shot by anti-fascist Italian partisans.
April 29– May 1, 1945	▶ The German forces in Italy surrender.

resistance was fierce, but after three weeks, the major southern city of Naples had fallen.

HARD FIGHTING

The Germans established a strong defensive line across Italy—the Gustav Line, about 100 miles (160 km) south of Rome. Fighting in difficult terrain, the Allies' advance stalled, and they began a long and grueling struggle to capture Monte Cassino, a famous mountain monastery fortified by the Germans. In an attempt to outflank the Germans, the Allies landed north of the Gustav Line at Anzio, only to be pinned down there for months.

Finally, Polish troops stormed Monte Cassino, the Gustav Line was broken, and the Allies entered Rome on June 4, 1944. The Germans fell back on the equally strongly fortified Gothic Line. By this time, the Allied invasion of France was being reinforced by units taken from Italy—now seen as a "sideshow." Despite some intense fighting, the Italian campaign ended only in April 1945, when Axis resistance was crumbling everywhere.

After a daring, glider-borne rescue by Nazi special forces, the fallen Italian leader, Mussolini, boards a plane for Germany.

CROSS-REFERENCE FIGHTING ON BEACHES: PAGES 32–33

D-Day

The Allies' long-planned invasion of France, Operation Overlord, began with night drops of parachutists inland. Then, following a naval bombardment and air attacks, the first landings took place on the Normandy coast at 6:30 a.m. on June 6, 1944, known as D-day. Amphibious (land-and-sea) operations played a great part in World War II, but nothing compared with the 4,000 vessels and 11,000 aircraft assembled on D-day.

ON THE BEACHES

Within 24 hours, 156,000 U.S., British and Canadian troops had been landed on five beaches. All held on to their positions, although on "Omaha" beach the veteran U.S. First Infantry Division was pinned down for a time and badly mauled. Reinforcements poured in and artificial ("Mulberry") harbors were towed across the English Channel and used to deliver tanks and other equipment. The Germans had been misled into thinking the invasion would come at the Calais area to the north, and they were slow to regroup.

Even so, the five beachheads were only united into a single front on June 12. A fortnight later, the port of Cherbourg fell. But the real breakthrough came at the beginning of August, when the U.S. Third Army thrust into the neighboring province of Brittany and simultaneously broke

Normandy invaded: the sky is thick with parachutes as Allied units drop behind the German lines during the campaign.

Landing craft line "Omaha" beach, where Allied forces met the fiercest resistance.

| TIMELINE | FRANCE LIBERATED 1944 |

TIMELINE | FRANCE LIBERATED 1944

June 6, 1944 ▶ D-day: the Allies land on the Normandy coast.

June 12, 1944 ▶ The five Allied beachheads are united.

July 20, 1944 ▶ German officers fail in an attempt to kill Hitler and overthrow the Nazi regime.

July 31, 1944 ▶ U.S. troops take Avranches and break out of Normandy.

August 15, 1944 ▶ American and Free French troops land in the south of France.

August 21, 1944 ▶ The Allies close the "Falaise gap."

August 25, 1944 ▶ Paris is liberated as the Free French Second Armored Division enters the city.

September 11, 1944 ▶ Allied troops from Normandy and the south of France meet at Dijon.

September 30, 1944 ▶ Calais falls to the Allies, who have liberated almost all of France and Belgium.

out to the east, threatening to cut off a German army fighting the British and Canadians and falling back toward Falaise. When their counterattacks failed, the Germans fled through the rapidly closing "Falaise gap." Relentlessly pursued and pounded from the air, the Germans' Army Group B lost 10,000 men. Also, 50,000 men were made prisoners, and huge quantities of tanks and war materials were lost.

PARIS LIBERATED

With the Germans in full retreat, the Allies advanced rapidly, liberated Paris on August 25, and thrust into central France. They linked up with Allied forces advancing from southern France, but then, beginning to run short of fuel, slowed their advance. However, Germany was now under attack on all sides, and the end of the war seemed to be in sight.

CROSS-REFERENCE PARACHUTE DROPS: PAGES 40–41

"Chin-deep in the water"

"Unseen snipers concealed in the cliffs were shooting down at individuals, causing screams from those being hit. . . . **There were dead men floating in the water** and there were live men acting dead, letting the tide take them in. I was crouched down to chin-deep in the water. . . . I don't know how long we were in the water before the move was made, but I would guess close to an hour . . ."

Sergeant John Slaughter, age 19 on D-day, recalls what happened when he jumped from his landing craft on "Omaha" beach.
Quoted in Sean Sheehan, *Days That Shook the World: D-Day: 6th June 1944* (Wayland, 2002).

Assault on Saipan

On June 15, 1944, within a few days of the Normandy landings, 150 U.S. ships were delivering 127,000 men onto the beaches of a Pacific island. Saipan was one of the Marianas Islands, potential launchpads for further invasions or airfields from which the U.S.'s B-29 Superfortress bombers could reach Tokyo. The Japanese took the threat so seriously that they sent a powerful fleet against the Americans. But the Battle of the Philippine Sea turned into a disaster—a "turkey shoot" in which the Imperial Navy lost three carriers and 460 planes. So many pilots were killed that Japan's naval air arm never properly recovered. U.S. forces went on to land on Tinian and Guam, and also in the Marianas. The Japanese always refused to contemplate surrender, and on Saipan, 8,000 soldiers and civilians committed suicide rather than be captured. Some pockets of resistance survived for months, but the Americans went ahead and built their airfields.

A U.S. Marine discovers a Japanese family hiding in a cave from the fierce fighting on Saipan.

THE PHILIPPINES

In October 1944, U.S. forces struck in another sector. They invaded Leyte in the Philippines. The Japanese navy again tried to save the day. The Battle of Leyte Gulf was, in numbers, the greatest of all naval battles, involving 282 vessels. By now U.S. superiority was overwhelming, and the Japanese suffered a crushing defeat. But they produced dangerous new weapons— the kamikazes, suicide bombers who crashed their planes into U.S. vessels.

A Japanese warship sinking off Leyte island in the Philippines, having failed to prevent U.S. landings.

THE DECLINE OF JAPAN 1944–1945

June 3, 1944	▶ The Japanese retreat from India.
June 15, 1944	▶ U.S. forces land on Saipan; by mid-August, Saipan, Tinian, and Guam have been taken.
June 19–20, 1944	▶ The Battle of the Philippine Sea.
October 10, 1944	▶ The Americans land on Leyte, Philippines.
October 23, 1944	▶ The Battle of Leyte Gulf (second Battle of the Philippine Sea).
January 9, 1945	▶ Luzon is invaded.
February 19, 1945	▶ U.S. landing on Iwo Jima.
March 9, 1945	▶ 279 Superfortresses devastate Tokyo. Over 83,000 Japanese die in the air attacks.
April 1, 1945	▶ U.S. assault on Okinawa; most resistance ends by mid-June.
May 3, 1945	▶ Burma: the British Fourteenth Army captures Rangoon; the Japanese are in full retreat.

Bushido

The Japanese code of honor, Bushido, taught that a warrior must be willing to sacrifice himself and die rather than surrender. The Japanese treated Allied prisoners of war with great cruelty, believing they had behaved shamefully in not fighting to the death. The Japanese often attacked in a way that seemed suicidal to westerners. Toward the end of the war, when Japan was in dire straits, Japanese fliers called kamikazes piloted their bomb-filled planes like guided missiles, crashing them into U.S. ships. In every stronghold, Japanese soldiers fought almost to the last man. Huge numbers gave their lives pointlessly. U.S. casualties, though much smaller, were big enough to persuade the Americans to use the atomic bomb (page 44) rather than invade Japan itself.

JAPAN SUFFERS

The main Philippine island, Luzon, was invaded in January 1945, and a grim struggle followed. Meanwhile, other U.S. forces were thrusting directly toward Japan. Terrible, bloody conflicts took place before first Iwo Jima and then the larger island of Okinawa were taken.

Unable to defend itself by air or sea, Japan itself was now suffering. Carriers shelled the coast, and Superfortresses dropped unprecedented quantities of bombs on the cities. On March 9, 1945, the most devastating raid in history consumed central Tokyo and killed over 80,000 people. As the war in Europe ended, the Japanese braced themselves to meet an invasion.

CROSS-REFERENCE JAPAN SURRENDERS: PAGES 44–45

Great Red Army Offensive

22 JUNE 1944

The great Soviet summer offensive was timed to begin on June 22, 1944, the third anniversary of the Nazi invasion of the Soviet Union—a reminder of just how much the military situation had changed. After their defeats at Stalingrad and Kursk, the Germans had been steadily pushed back in 1943–1944. Leningrad had been relieved after a terrible thousand-day siege, and one by one Smolensk, Kiev, and other major cities were retaken. As in the West, Hitler's reluctance to permit withdrawals led to heavy losses of men and materials and made it harder for his armies to resist the growing strength of the Red Army.

halt. During the offensive, the Soviets overran Majdanek, a Nazi death camp that provided firsthand evidence of mass gassings and other horrors.

Red Army soldiers move through the debris of a strongly German-defended city.

THRUSTS AND HAMMER BLOWS

The new offensive began with a series of thrusts and hammer blows as the Red Army surged across the Dnieper River. It took Vitebsk and Minsk and shattered the German Army Group Center. Soviet troops crossed the prewar Polish frontier and on July 23 captured the German stronghold of Pinsk. Moving ahead quickly, they arrived within sight of the Vistula River and Warsaw.

Having covered 450 miles (725 km) in five weeks, the Soviets finally began to lose momentum. Their supply lines had become overextended, while German resistance was stiffening. For the time being, the advance came to a

Celebrating victories

"In Moscow today all hearts are filled with joy. Every night, sometimes once, sometimes twice, sometimes even three times, a familiar deep male voice . . . announces a new major victory, and then ten minutes later guns boom and thousands of coloured rockets light up the night and the summer sky. It is always much the same spectacle, but it remains equally thrilling. . . . Every night, **in millions of Russian houses,** *little paper flags and pieces of coloured string and red pencils mark off more large slices of Soviet territory liberated from the enemy."*

A British war correspondent in the USSR, Alexander Werth, records the jubilant mood. Quoted in Henning Krabbe, ed., *Voices from Britain: Broadcast History 1939–1945* (Allen and Unwin, 1947).

RED ARMY TRIUMPHS

Though stalled outside Warsaw, the Red Amy remained on the offensive in other sectors. From August 1944, battles raged in the Baltic states (Lithuania, Latvia, and Estonia). They were secured by the end of the year, opening the way for an invasion of East Prussia, German territory north of Poland.

Germany's allies were now falling away. Finland asked the Soviet Union for an armistice. Soviet offensives in the Balkans led Romania and Bulgaria to change sides and declare war on Germany. The Germans evacuated Greece, and partisans and the Red Army liberated the Yugoslav capital, Belgrade. Soon it would be the turn of Germany itself.

Homeless people in the streets of Minsk (now the capital of Belarus). Their houses have been burned down by the retreating Germans.

CROSS-REFERENCE GERMAN COLLAPSE: PAGES 42–43

Warsaw Uprising

By late July 1944, the Red Army was approaching the Polish capital, Warsaw. Despite Nazi oppression, the Poles had managed to create a secret resistance force, the Home Army. Believing that Soviet help was at hand, 40,000 Home Army soldiers rose on August 1 and seized Warsaw.

FIGHTING AGAINST THE ODDS

The Germans were shaken by the uprising, but since the Red Army remained inactive, they brought in reinforcements against the Poles. The fighting was prolonged, yet still no Soviet help arrived. The Red Army offensive had stalled, but even token assistance was lacking. The Soviet dictator, Stalin, was almost certainly glad to see the Germans destroy an independent force that might oppose his plans for postwar Poland. Supplies were flown in from Britain and Allied-occupied Italy, but they were too far away to give effective help.

Outgunned and outnumbered, the Home Army resisted for 63 days. The Germans had to drive them back house by house; they fought in the cellars and even moved from place to place via the sewers. They were finally forced to surrender on October 2. German massacres of civilians during the fighting meant that the rising cost 250,000 lives. After it, Hitler ordered the complete destruction of Warsaw.

RESISTANCE TO TYRANNY

The Warsaw Uprising was a dramatic example of resistance to the Nazis in occupied Europe. Everywhere hatred of the Nazis was intensified by their barbaric behavior. Inspired by Hitler's

At the end of their tether: men of the Polish Home Army, wounded in the Rising, face the inevitability of defeat and capture.

Into the sewers

"We entered the sewer from Krashinski Square. . . . The water rushed by so strongly that we had to hold on to each other. . . . The darkness was periodically illuminated by the leader's lantern. **The water roared and emitted a frightful stench.** People who fainted were carried away. . . . But then we found ourselves under the Cracow Faubourg, which was patrolled by Germans, who from time to time threw in hand grenades. . . . At last we reached the manhole by Varka Street . . . and we breathed fresh air."

A resistance fighter recalls his daring but dirty escape. Quoted in Norman Davies, *Rising '44: The Battle for Warsaw* (Macmillan, 2003).

race theories, the Germans enslaved and degraded the Poles. Soviet prisoners of war were worked to death, and Jews in Eastern Europe were massacred. Then, from 1942, the killings became systematic, and Jews and other victims from all over Europe were transported to camps such as Auschwitz and gassed; in all, some 6 million Jews are thought to have perished. In western Europe, men were forced to work in Germany to keep its industries going, and resistance was punished by killing hostages or massacring entire villages.

CROSS-REFERENCE
WAR CRIMES:
PAGES 34–35, 44–45

Although some people collaborated (cooperated) with the Germans, Nazi terror generally provoked rather than stifled resistance. In many countries, the underground (secret resisters) carried out acts of sabotage, and groups or armies of partisans (open resisters) fought guerrilla campaigns against the Axis in southern France, Greece, and Yugoslavia. They could not liberate themselves without help, but Europeans showed by their actions that they rejected fascist tyranny.

Polish men and women, carrying their few possessions, are marched out of Warsaw on their way to concentration camps.

Battle of the Bulge Begins

Help arrives for the besieged Allied forces in Bastogne. A U.S. patrol passes a row of ruined houses in the town.

By late 1944, the Allies were quietly confident of victory. After the rapid liberation of France, they had had a setback when Montgomery attempted a thrust through the Netherlands, intended to outflank the German defenses and end the war in one blow. His army made slow headway, and airborne forces, dropped behind enemy lines to secure river crossings, risked being trapped. The farthest away were the British and Polish at Arnhem, under attack from two panzer divisions. They fought with great gallantry, but only a quarter of the 10,000 "Red Devils" escaped death or capture.

HITLER'S GAMBLE

Nevertheless, the Allies were taken completely by surprise when, on December 16, the Germans launched a full-scale counteroffensive. During a lull in the fighting, the German generals had managed to rebuild their armies and consolidate their defenses. But Hitler had decided on a final gamble. As in 1940, German armies would break through the Ardennes, drive the Allies back, and retake the

"Nuts!"

During the Battle of the Bulge, U.S. paratroops were dropped into the market town of Bastogne, at the junction of some important roads. They were joined by other U.S. units but soon found themselves trapped by the advancing Germans. The Americans held out doggedly, though they were outnumbered and running short of ammunition. When the Germans suggested that they should surrender, the American commander, Anthony C. McAuliffe, gave a single-word reply that became famous: "Nuts!" A day later, the skies cleared and supplies were dropped. And on December 26, American tanks drove through the German lines, creating a relief corridor, maintained until the Germans were driven out of the area.

Belgian port of Antwerp. Twenty-four German divisions poured through the snow-covered forests, a thinly defended front where many of the U.S. troops were raw recruits. They resisted courageously, but the weight of armor and surprise were on the Germans' side.

THE GAMBLE FAILS

The Germans' rapid progress created a large bulge (salient) in the front line, which gave the battle its name as the Allies brought up reinforcements and attacked it. The German advance slowed as the balance of forces changed and the weather improved, allowing Allied air superiority to take effect. German commanders knew that Antwerp was an unrealistic target but hoped to reach the River Meuse. On Christmas Day, as they came in sight of it, their fuel supplies ran out. In other sectors, the "bulge" was already under attack. The panzers were steadily forced back, and by late January, the Allies were again on the German frontier, poised to invade. Hitler's final gamble had failed, squandering men and materials sorely needed for the defense of the beleaguered fatherland.

CROSS-REFERENCE COUNTERATTACKS: PAGES 28–29

U.S. airborne troops advance through the snow as the Allies regain the initiative in the hard-fought Battle of the Bulge.

Battle for Berlin Begins

An earsplitting early morning bombardment announced the beginning of the end for Adolf Hitler and Nazism. The Red Army stood poised to assault the German capital and capture or kill the Führer himself.

The Battle for Berlin marked the climax of a Soviet offensive launched on January 12. After months of re-forming and resupplying, the Soviets struck with overwhelming force. Warsaw and Budapest fell, and the Red Army forged ahead on all fronts, liberating Poland and making significant advances into Germany itself. By March, they had reached the Oder River, only 50 miles (80 km) from Berlin. The Germans inflicted heavy casualties on the Soviets, but Stalin now scented victory and his armies were soon on the move again.

ASSAULT ON HITLER'S CAPITAL

Within a day of starting the April offensive, the Red Army had established bridgeheads across the

A shattered Reichstag (parliament building) stands amid the ruins of Berlin, surrounded by the forces of the victors.

The balance of forces and the human cost

	Armed forces at peak strength (millions)	Military deaths	Civilian deaths°
ALLIES			
Britain	4.60	326,000	62,000
China	5.00	3,000,000	7,000,000
Commonwealth	3.90	196,500	1,700,000
France	5.00	212,000	267,000
Poland	1.00	400,000	5,300,000
U.S.	12.36	295,000	11,200
Soviet Union*	12.50	8,600,000	7,000,000
AXIS			
Germany	10.00	3,300,000	2,300,000
Italy	4.50	330,000	80,000
Japan	6.00	1,500,000	600,000

* Soviet military figures include murdered prisoners of war. ° Civilian deaths include merchant seamen.

Oder and Neisse. The German Ninth and Fourth Armies were flung back, and by April 24, Soviet troops were in the suburbs of Berlin. The Germans had still managed to muster a million troops to defend the capital, although some were recently conscripted old men and pathetically young boys. The Soviet forces were 2.5 million strong, backed by thousands of tanks, artillery pieces, and aircraft. The struggle was hopeless, but Hitler refused to leave or to contemplate surrender.

THE DEATH OF HITLER

Berlin was encircled, and a street-by-street battle developed in which artillery, tanks, and flamethrowers completed the ruin of the city. Hitler and his staff now lived in a bunker under the Reich Chancellery (his official residence). When Soviet troops were just a few hundred yards away, Hitler realized that the end had come. Having ordered terrible atrocities, he had no intention of being captured. He married his longtime companion Eva Braun and dictated his self-justifying Political Testament. The following day, April 30, he shot himself, Braun took poison, and their bodies were burned. The Berlin garrison surrendered, and in a few days all German resistance ended. The war in Europe was over.

CROSS-REFERENCE
ENCIRCLED CITIES: PAGES 14–15, 28–29

May 1945: on Lüneburg Heath in Germany, Field Marshall Montgomery reads the terms of surrender to a German military delegation.

Hiroshima Destroyed

On August 6, 1945, at 2:45 a.m., a B-29 bomber, the *Enola Gay*, left the Pacific island of Tinian carrying a single bomb. By 8:15, the aircraft was flying above the industrial city of Hiroshima. It dropped the bomb, and at 8:16, when it was falling toward its target, a radar signal detonated it.

DAY OF TERROR

There was a gigantic flash of light and a terrible blast. Thousands were killed instantly, their bodies vanishing or turning into fragile statues of ash. More deaths followed as a shock wave flattened houses and loosed storms of brick, metal and glass fragments. Fires raged all over the city, which was filled with burned, dead, and dying people. An enormous mushroom cloud rose above Hiroshima and blotted out the light. Later, as the cloud cooled, filthy black rain fell.

About 80,000 people were killed instantly, and tens of thousands died of their injuries or the aftereffects of radiation. Hiroshima had been destroyed by a terrifying new weapon, the atomic bomb, based on the immense energy released when the nucleus (core) of an atom is split or fused with another nucleus. "The Bomb" had been developed by an international team of scientists at Los Alamos, New Mexico. It was not ready when the war in Europe ended, and the decision to use it against Japan was, and remains, controversial. One important motive for doing so was the belief that

The huge "mushroom" cloud created by the first atomic bomb.

invading Japan would result in huge casualties on both sides. Instead the war could be ended immediately with one or two shattering blows.

WAR'S END

On August 8, the Soviet Union declared war and its forces poured into Manchuria. A day later, a second

TIMELINE	"THE BOMB" 1938–1945
December 1938	▶ Two German scientists, Otto Hahn and Fritz Strassman, split the nucleus of an atom.
October 10, 1939	▶ President Roosevelt receives a letter from world-famous scientist Albert Einstein, alerting him to the possibility of an atomic bomb.
1941	▶ Serious research on making an atomic bomb begins in Chicago. Later the project moves to Los Alamos.
July 16, 1945	▶ An atomic bomb is successfully tested in the New Mexican desert.
July 25, 1945	▶ President Truman authorizes the use of the bomb against Japan.
August 6, 1945	▶ Hiroshima is destroyed.
August 9, 1945	▶ Nagasaki is A-bombed.
August 14, 1945	▶ The Japanese accept the Allies' terms.
September 2, 1945	▶ Japan signs formal surrender documents on the USS *Missouri*.

After the bomb fell: a single building, now preserved as a memorial, remains standing in the city center of Hiroshima.

atomic bomb was dropped on Nagasaki. Though Japan's position was hopeless, the military still hesitated. The emperor, Hirohito, normally stayed out of politics, but at a meeting of the Supreme War Council, he cast his vote for surrender. The Allied terms were accepted, and World War II came to an end.

CROSS-REFERENCE CAPITULATIONS: PAGES 8–9, 18–19, 28–29, 42–43

After the war

As the war ended, the United Nations was founded in the hope of maintaining world peace. Occupied Germany was divided into four zones: American, British, French and Soviet. Japan was occupied by the U.S. Leading Nazis were tried at Nuremberg in Germany for war crimes. Many were hanged or sentenced to imprisonment. Similar trials were held in Japan.

The U.S. and the Soviet Union emerged as the two postwar superpowers. They soon came into conflict, and U.S.- and Soviet-led alliances faced off in a "Cold War." Nuclear weapons far more destructive than the A-bomb were developed, but, to the relief of a fearful world, they had not been used when the Cold War ended with the collapse of the Soviet Union in 1991.

Key Figures in World War II

WINSTON CHURCHILL (1874–1965), BRITISH STATESMAN AND WRITER

During a long political career, Churchill held many ministerial posts. By the 1930s, his career seemed over, but his warnings against Nazi Germany proved justified and he became prime minister in May 1940. His stirring speeches and fighting spirit made him a great leader. Unexpectedly defeated in the 1945 general election, he was prime minister again from 1951 to 1955.

DWIGHT D. EISENHOWER (1890–1969), U.S. GENERAL

Eisenhower commanded the Allied invasion of Algeria (French North Africa) in November 1942. He became supreme Allied commander for the 1944 invasion of Europe launched on D-Day. After the war he served as U.S. president from 1953 to 1959.

CHARLES DE GAULLE (1890–1970), FRENCH GENERAL

After the fall of France in 1940, de Gaulle escaped to London and set up a Free French government and army to carry on the war. After the liberation, he was briefly president in 1945. In May 1958, he took power again, founded the Fifth French Republic, and served as president until April 1969.

ADOLF HITLER (1889–1945), GERMAN DICTATOR

Hitler was born in Austria but fought in the German army during World War I. After becoming leader of the Nazi Party, he led a failed revolt in 1923 and was briefly imprisoned. His book *Mein Kampf* ("My Struggle") presents extreme nationalist and racist policies that were carried out when he became German Führer (leader) in 1933. His foreign policy and military decisions achieved unexpected successes but, as he lost touch with reality, finally brought disaster.

BERNARD MONTGOMERY (1887–1976), BRITISH MILITARY COMMANDER

Montgomery led the Eighth Army to victory at El Alamein in North Africa and then in Sicily and southern Italy. Despite his poor relations with American commanders, he played an important role in the 1944 Normandy landings, Battle of the Bulge, and invasion of Germany.

BENITO MUSSOLINI (1883–1945), ITALIAN DICTATOR

Mussolini took power in 1922 and turned Italy into a fascist state. The regime's dismal wartime performance led to his downfall in 1943. Rescued from prison by the Germans, he headed a revived fascist state in northern Italy. When that collapsed, he fled but was captured and shot by partisans.

ERWIN ROMMEL (1891–1944), GERMAN MILITARY COMMANDER

Rommel was the brilliantly successful commander of the Afrika Korps in North Africa until his defeat at El Alamein. In February 1944, he was put in charge of German defenses on the Atlantic coast but failed to prevent the D-day landings. He was badly wounded in July 1944. Suspected of involvement in the plot to kill Hitler, he shot himself to spare his family persecution, allowing the Nazis to pretend that he had died heroically of his injuries.

FRANKLIN D. ROOSEVELT (1882–1945), 32ND U.S. PRESIDENT

Roosevelt took office in 1933, at the height of the Depression, a worldwide economic crisis that he tackled with the "New Deal," involving vigorous government action. Although disabled by polio, he was re-elected a record three times and led the U.S. until his death in April 1945, just before the end of the war.

JOSEPH STALIN (1879–1953), SOVIET DICTATOR

Stalin was one of the leaders of the 1917 October Revolution that set up a communist regime. By the late 1920s, he had eliminated all his rivals. He launched a program of rapid industrialization to make the Soviet Union a great power. But his rule was also accompanied by mass arrests and executions of real and imaginary opponents. His wartime leadership was typically ruthless and successful, and he remained in power until his death.

Glossary

Allies the countries, including Britain, the U.S. and the Soviet Union, that fought against the Axis

appeasement Anglo-French policy of making concessions to Hitler and Mussolini

armistice a truce, usually before a surrender or peace

Axis Germany, Italy, Japan, and their allies

beachhead area of a beach on which an invader lands troops and equipment

demilitarized describes a territory in which no armed forces are allowed

fascism set of political ideas favoring military-style societies that glorify war and all-powerful leaders

guerrilla warfare hit-and-run warfare, usually waged by the weaker side in a conflict

incendiaries bombs designed to start fires when they hit the ground

Luftwaffe German air force

Nazi Party The National Socialist Party, led by Hitler, which ruled Germany 1933–1945

partisans civilians who took up arms and fought as guerrillas against fascism

pincer movement tactic of advancing on both sides of an enemy, intending to surround it

protectorate state or territory "protected" against other powers by a stronger state; the "protection" may really be domination

puppet state supposedly independent state that is actually controlled by another state

radar method of identifying distant objects (e.g., planes) by radio pulses

sabotage destruction of equipment, etc., by people acting secretly

salient bulge in a front line, vulnerable to attack from several directions

saturation bombing bombing that destroys a large area rather than specific targets

sonar device to locate submarines using sound waves

sortie attack followed by a return to base

strafing raking people on the ground with machine-gun fire from a plane

U-boat German submarine

underground secret movement that works to overthrow a regime

Further Information

BOOKS

Connolly, Sean, *World War II*. Heinemann, 2003.

Harris, Nathaniel, *Hiroshima*. Heinemann, 2004.

Harris, Nathaniel, *Pearl Harbor*. Dryad, 1986.

Harris, Nathaniel, *The Rise of Hitler*. Heinemann, 2004.

Marston, Daniel ed. *The Pacific War Companion: From Pearl Harbor to Hiroshima*. Osprey, 2005.

Reynoldson, Fiona. *Key Battles of World War Two*. Heinemann, 2002.

Ross, Stewart. *The Blitz*. Evans, 2002.

WEBSITES

www.bbc.co.uk/history/worldwars/wwtwo/
A very good starting point: accessibly written, with well-designed interactive and animated features

http://www.schoolshistory.org.uk/secondworldwar.htm
Nicely broken down into subjects and with generally clear explanations

http://www.channel4.com/history/microsites/W/ww2weapons/
Especially good for those interested in the military and technological aspects of the war

www.historyplaces.com/unitedstates/pacificwar/index.hmtl
A photo gallery of the Pacific War, with very memorable images; a good point from which to explore other parts of the History Place site

PLACES TO VISIT

Imperial War Museum, London

Army Museum, London

D-Day Museum, Portsmouth

Musée de la Paix, Caen, Normandy, France

National World War II Museum, New Orleans

Index

Numbers in **bold** refer to photographs or, where indicated, to maps.